Dear Parent:
Your child's love of reading starts here!

Every child learns to read in a different way and at his or her own speed. Some go back and forth between reading levels and read favorite books again and again. Others read through each level in order. You can help your young reader improve and become more confident by encouraging his or her own interests and abilities. From books your child reads with you to the first books he or she reads alone, there are I Can Read Books for every stage of reading:

SHARED READING
Basic language, word repetition, and whimsical illustrations, ideal for sharing with your emergent reader

BEGINNING READING
Short sentences, familiar words, and simple concepts for children eager to read on their own

READING WITH HELP
Engaging stories, longer sentences, and language play for developing readers

READING ALONE
Complex plots, challenging vocabulary, and high-interest topics for the independent reader

ADVANCED READING
Short paragraphs, chapters, and exciting themes for the perfect bridge to chapter books

I Can Read Books have introduced children to the joy of reading since 1957. Featuring award-winning authors and illustrators and a fabulous cast of beloved characters, I Can Read Books set the standard for beginning readers.

A lifetime of discovery begins with the magical words "I Can Read!"

Visit www.icanread.com for information
on enriching your child's reading experience.

WHAT A GOOD KITTY

BY MERCER MAYER

HARPER

An Imprint of HarperCollinsPublishers

For Eric and Amanda Christenson
and
their new baby!!

I Can Read Book® is a trademark of HarperCollins Publishers.

Little Critter: What a Good Kitty

Library of Congress card number: 2011941958
ISBN 978-0-06-083566-8 (trade bdg.)—ISBN 978-0-06-083565-1 (pbk.)
Typography by Diane Dubreuil
12 13 14 15 16   SCP   10 9 8 7 6 5 4 3 2 1   ❖   First Edition

A Big Tuna Trading Company, LLC/J.R. Sansevere Book
www.littlecritter.com

I have a good kitty.

She likes to sleep.

I like to play.

She likes to play.

We play chase.

My kitty is hard to catch.

I trick her with some milk.

Then I catch my kitty.

She messes up my dad's newspaper.

Dad says, "Bad kitty!"

My kitty messes up Mom's knitting.
Mom says, "Bad, bad kitty!"

My kitty is messy.
She messes up my
little sister's dolls.

My little sister says,
"Bad, bad, bad kitty."

My kitty spills Blue's food.

Blue barks, "Woof, woof."

My kitty runs away.

She scares the fish.
She spills the trash
with a loud, loud crash.

Oh, no! My kitty is in big trouble

Dad puts my kitty outside.

My kitty is mad.

She runs up a tree.

The tree is very tall.

My kitty can't get down.

She cries and cries.

Dad feels bad and climbs the tree.

But he can't reach my kitty.

Dad gets stuck, too.

Mom calls the fire department.
They come with a big fire truck.

Fireman Joe saves my kitty
and my dad.

Dad is not happy with my kitty.

Mom is not happy with my kitty.

Little Sister is not happy
with my kitty.
My kitty is sad.

I play with my kitty.
Little Sister plays
in the sandbox.

She is still mad.

A big mean dog
comes in our yard
and growls at Little Sister.

Little Sister is scared.

I am, too.

My kitty is brave.

She scares the mean dog away.

Dad says, "What a good kitty!"

Mom says, "What a good kitty!"

Little Sister says,

"What a good kitty!"

I knew that.